The rules presented in this book are for informational purposes only. Beca[...]
should evaluate your particular situation and consult a professional dog expe[...]

Dedicated to my son CJ and my dog Melbi
that are the source of my inspiration!

ACKNOWLEDGMENTS
A special thank you to my wonderful husband, Cesare Peraglie,
for always being supportive.
I also want to express my appreciation and gratitude to
Mrs. Flo Ballengee, Mrs. Diana Lopresti and Mrs. Marita Sunnarborg
for their feedback and support.
I want to thank all my friends for their enthusiasm for my book.

CONTENTS

1. At the dog shelter

One day CJ and Sofia asked Mom and Dad for a special present: a puppy!
Mom said that a dog is a big commitment.
"We need to consider if we have enough time for a dog. A puppy has to be walked every day, he needs to be trained and socialized. We also need to take into account the cost of food, grooming and medical expenses!" Mom said.
"You never had a pet and before bringing a dog into our home, we need to see how you behave around dogs," Daddy said.

Several days later Dad said, "We are going to a dog shelter to meet Mrs. Dianne. She is an old friend of mine and she will teach us how to interact with dogs."
During the drive, the kids were preparing questions for Mrs. Dianne and explaining to their parents how much they wanted a dog.
Mrs. Dianne was very nice and explained that everybody needs to follow rules when meeting new dogs. "Here are the rules!" she said giving the children a small brochure.

Rules when you meet a new dog

- *Always ask the owner for permission to pet the dog.*
- *Get close to the dog slowly and let him sniff your hand.*
- *If he is a small dog, squat down to the dog's level so he will not be scared.*
- *Don't bend over a dog or put your hand over the dog's head because the dog can see it as a threatening gesture and bite you.*
- *Don't pet the dog on the back because the dog could have pain in that area and he can show you that he doesn't like it.*
- *Pet the dog under his chin.*
- *Don't be too noisy.*
- *Don't try to kiss or put your face close to any animal.*
- *Don't look a dog in the eyes because this may frighten him and he may react with aggression.*
- *Never pet a dog behind a fence or a chained dog because he can be frustrated by the situation and react aggressively.*

After Mrs. Dianne explained the rules, the group decided that it was time to meet some of the dogs.

Sofia was unsure and she asked, "What am I supposed to do if I am scared?"

Mrs. Dianne answered that the best things to do if you are scared are:

- *Take deep breaths, try to relax and ask for the help of a grownup.*
- *Don't turn and run away because the dog may chase you.*

- *Don't look a dog in the eyes because the dog may think that it is a sign of aggression.*

Then CJ wanted to know what to do in case a dog *jumps* on him.
Mrs. Dianne explained, *"If the dog is small, stand still and don't react. Dogs jump because they want your attention. If you don't pay attention to them, the jumping will stop. If the dog is big, do the same but move close to a wall or a sofa so that you don't fall.* Now let's meet Yack."

Yack was a beautiful mid-sized brown dog and was really excited to see new people. His way to greet was leaping up on everybody. Mrs. Dianne showed how to make him stop. She didn't make eye contact but she looked directly over his head ignoring him. At one point she also turned away from him. Basically her body language showed him that she wasn't interested in greeting him that way. Once Yack's four paws were on the ground, she gave him a treat and a lot of praise. She then invited the children to do the same. Yack was a smart dog and very soon he realized that he was rewarded only when he was not jumping.
CJ and Sofia had a lot of fun with him and they went home very happy and with the desire to learn more about dogs.

If a dog jumps on you,
Staying still is the best thing to do!

2. At the park

The next weekend the family decided to walk to a nearby park and have a picnic.

On the way to the park, Sofia started complaining, "Mom, I am tired."

"You need to get used to walking if you want a dog. I know very little about dogs but there is one thing I know for sure: dogs need to walk at least twenty minutes a day," replied Mom.

"The dog can run in our backyard," suggested Sofia.

"I think a dog needs to walk on a leash because this creates a bond with the owner and it is better exercise for the dog," said Dad.

Just before arriving at the park, they saw a dog behind a fence. Sofia got closer and closer until Dad exclaimed, " Remember what Mrs. Dianne said! *Never pet a dog behind a fence or a chained dog because he can be frustrated by the situation and react aggressively.*"

"Dad is right. Sofia please step back. Safety first!" Mom added.

Behind a fence,
A dog can be too tense!

After the picnic lunch Mom and Sofia were reading a book and CJ and Dad were playing soccer when a young lady walked by with a puppy.

"May I pet your dog?" asked CJ.

After the girl said yes, CJ slowly got close to the dog, let the dog sniff his hand and then started petting him under his chin.

The young lady explained that meeting new people was very good for her dog. " My dog Cippi needs to be socialized."

"What does socialized mean?" asked CJ.

"Socialization means that Cippi needs to meet other dogs and people and be comfortable in unfamiliar situations. This will prevent him from becoming shy, fearful and potentially aggressive."

When you meet someone else's pet,
Meet it with a lot of respect!

3. At a friend's house

One day at school CJ received an invitation for a play date. He was very excited to go to his friend Joshy's house to play, especially because he knew that Joshy had a dog.

During the drive, CJ was thinking about the rules that Mrs. Dianne told him to follow when meeting a new dog. Do *not touch, do not talk, no eye contact* (1) *and let the dog sniff you and then quietly pet the dog under the chin.*

CJ rang the bell. He heard Mickey, Joshy's dog, bark and he heard Joshy give him the command *Sit/Stay* before opening the door. When CJ went inside he saw Mickey sitting still.

"That is so cool!" exclaimed CJ.

Then Joshy released the dog with the word O.K. and Mickey started greeting CJ by sniffing him but not jumping. After CJ pet Mickey under his chin, he asked Joshy where he learned to train his dog.

"Last year we had some problems with Mickey so we had a dog trainer teach us what to do. The lesson was once a week but he also gave us exercises to do during the week. After a few sessions, Mickey was much more obedient. If you want, I can show you some tricks!"

Joshy then showed CJ what the dog trainer taught him. CJ was very impressed.

(1)   Cesar Millan, The Dog Whisperer TV show

After playing with video games for a while the boys decided to change activities.

CJ said, "Let's play super heroes!" and he grabbed a toy sword. Joshy grasped a broom and they started to run around and pretend to fight each other. They were very loud and Joshy's mom arrived and moved Mickey to another room.

Then she said, "Joshy you forgot about our rules. Your friend also doesn't know them so let's read them together."

She walked to the refrigerator where the rules were attached so the whole family could see them. She then started to read.

Rules when you have a dog

- *Don't bother your dog when he is sleeping or eating.*
- *Don't pull the dog's ears, tail, fur or any other part.*
- *If you play wrestling games with your friends, or with brooms, swords and sticks or you are too noisy, go in another room and close the door. Dogs can interpret the play like a dangerous situation and react.*
- *Dogs are not toys so don't ride your dog and don't try to dress him with doll outfits.*
- *If your dog has a special toy, don't grab it from his mouth.*
- *Don't try to kiss or put your face close to your dog.*

If you play with sticks and a broom,
Please go in another room!

Then she explained that Mickey was scared by the boy's playing and he was hiding under an armchair. CJ and Joshy said that they were sorry. Joshy's mom added, "For your safety it is not good to play rough when there are dogs around. Now let's sit down and have a snack before CJ's mom arrives. Do you want chocolate chip cookies and milk?"

"Yes," said the very excited boys.

"Just remember: don't give the cookies to Mickey because chocolate is very toxic for dogs."

4. A guest

Several days before Thanksgiving CJ and Sofia's mom announced, "We are going to have a guest! Mrs. Marita is going on a trip and she asked us to take care of her dog for a week. Are you willing to help me with Roxy?"

"Yes," exclaimed the children.

Finally Roxy arrived and Mrs. Marita explained, " Roxy eats half of a can of wet food mixed with some dry food and some pumpkin puree."

"Pumpkin puree?" asked CJ.

"Yes, pumpkin is really good for humans and dogs. It has a lot of fiber and vitamins," explained Mrs. Marita.

"I like pumpkin in a pumpkin pie!" exclaimed Sofia.

Mrs. Marita also showed the family the dog's favorite toys and how to play fetch. At the end she took the crate from the car.

"Do we need to put Roxy in this cage?" asked a worried Sofia.

Mrs. Marita smiled and said, "A lot of people see the crate in a negative way but actually it is a useful tool for housetraining and for preventing bad behavior. For example, when I am not able to supervise Roxy, her crate is a safe place for her to stay. She is very curious and the crate will prevent her from exploring around the house and from getting into trouble. The crate can also be a relaxing spot to take a nap, to chew a toy or enjoy time on her own when my children are too noisy. Having her accustomed to stay in a crate makes car and airplane trips less stressful. Leave the crate door open and you will see Roxy go in by herself. "

Mrs. Marita was right. When she left, Roxy sniffed around for a while and then she laid down in her crate until dinner time.

CJ offered to prepare Roxy's dinner. He put equal parts of wet and dry food in Roxy's bowl and, after having Roxy sit and stay, he put the bowl on the floor. Roxy started eating but very soon CJ realized that he forgot the pumpkin puree. As soon as CJ got close to her, Roxy showed him her teeth. CJ remembered one of the rules that he learned at Joshy's house: *Don't bother your dog when he is eating.*

It is not good,
To touch the dog's food!

For the next few days, CJ and Sofia played a lot with Roxy. With their parents help they found online instructions for fun games to play with dogs.

In the backyard, their favorite game was fetch. In the house, they liked playing hide and seek. One would stay with Roxy in one room while the other would hide in a different room. After being found by the dog, the child rewarded her with treats and praise.

CJ and Sofia always wanted to go with mom to walk Roxy. The walk was good exercise for everybody and was a good way to bond with the dog. One day they walked to the dog park and the children really enjoyed watching Roxy play with the other dogs. The only thing that they didn't like about the walk was cleaning up Roxy's poop. Mom explained the importance of keeping the town clean and that, in order to have a dog, they needed to take turns even in the less desirable jobs.

When Mrs. Marita arrived to take Roxy home, she was very pleased to know that the family enjoyed having her dog for a week.

Mom said, "We want to thank you for letting Roxy stay with us. We had a lot of fun and she helped CJ and Sofia learn the responsibilities of having a pet. Now I am sure that they are responsible enough to have a dog for Christmas."

" I found Roxy under the Christmas tree four years ago. She was a super cute puppy. Unfortunately, she ate some grapes that my children left on the floor. Because grapes are toxic for dogs, we had to spend Christmas Day at the veterinarian's office," said Mrs. Marita.

5. Back to the dog shelter

"Welcome back!" said Mrs. Dianne.

"We are here to find a puppy!" exclaimed a very excited Sofia.

"At the moment, we don't have puppies. The youngest is a one-year-old Spaniel/Chihuahua mix," replied Mrs. Dianne.

"We are a little bit concerned with adult dogs. We don't know if they were abused in the past and if they were, they could have behavioral problems," said Mom.

"Almost all the dogs in our shelter are not here because they have problems, but simply because they did not fit the lifestyle of their previous family or because their previous owner was not able to sustain the cost of having a dog. In this economic downturn, unfortunately, a lot of people lose their jobs," explained Mrs. Dianne.

"But puppies are so cute!" insisted Sofia.

"Having a puppy is almost like having a newborn baby. You need to housetrain him," said Mrs. Dianne.

"What does housetrain mean?" asked CJ.

"Housetraining means teaching your dog to pee and poop in his toilet area," explained Mrs. Dianne.

"How many times a day do we need to walk a three-month-old puppy to the toilet area?" asked Dad.

"Around eight times a day. The puppy should not remain in his crate for more than two hours during housetraining. The older the dog, the longer he can wait to relieve himself," answered Mrs. Dianne.

"With our schedule, this could be a problem," remarked Mom.

"Also puppies between four and six months of age have a very high activity level. Their energy reaches the highest point at around eight months. In addition, they want to be more independent and they may start to test the boundaries and the rules that they have accepted before," added Mrs. Dianne.

"Exactly like the kids!" exclaimed Dad.

"In addition, you need to decide if you want a pure or a mixed breed dog and what size you prefer," added Mrs. Dianne.

" I think we have a lot of things to think about," said Mom.

"Here. Take this book with you. Also you can look online and find a lot of important information," concluded Mrs. Dianne.

6. The final decision

Several weeks later, the family was sitting at the table eating dinner and they started to talk about dogs and about what they learned reading Mrs. Dianne's book.

Sofia said, "I would like to have a small white dog with long hair that I can brush and decorate with pink bows."

CJ wanted a short haired, big black dog.

" If you want a dog for Christmas, you need to compromise and find one that works for both of you," said Dad.

After a couple of days, CJ and Sofia talked with Mom and Dad. "We really want a dog but maybe it is a good idea to wait until after Christmas. During the holidays we are always so busy and excited. We have guests and a lot of new toys to play with," CJ said.

"We are scared that we won't have enough time for the dog," Sofia added.

"Spring break will be the perfect time to have a dog because there is no school and we have a lot of time to play and to train him," they remarked.

Dad said, "We agree and we are sure that, when the time is right, you will be very responsible dog owners!"

7. Quiz

Answer yes or no to the questions and find the solutions and the explanations at page 26.

1. Is it acceptable to dress your dog with dog outfits?

2. Is it o.k. to pet a dog that you already know without the owner's permission?

3. Is it true that the majority of the dogs at the shelter have behavioral problems?

4. Can your dog have a piece of your chocolate birthday cake?

5. Can your dog play wrestling games with you and your friends?

8. Glossary of terms

Abused dog A dog treated with cruelty or violence.

Behavioral problems An action that creates problems. It can be a behavior that is annoying to the owner (i.e. barking, jumping, chewing and digging) or a more dangerous behavior such as aggression against people or other dogs.

Body language It is a non-verbal form of communication that includes your posture, movement, gestures, facial expressions and eye contact. It is an important part of communication with dogs.

Breed A group of dogs with similar qualities.

Crate A box that keeps your dog inside. For small dogs, it could be a simple cardboard box. For big dogs, it is more like a cage. Your dog can use it as a den where he can sleep or relax. It is also useful for traveling, for housetraining and for preventing your dog from getting into trouble when you cannot supervise him.

Dog trainer A professional that helps a dog to become a well-behaved member of a family.

Dog shelter An organization that takes care of abandoned dogs and finds a new home for them.

Fetch A game that consists of throwing a ball, having your dog get the ball and return it back to you.

Grooming Taking care of a dog by brushing and bathing him, by trimming his nails and brushing his teeth.

Hide and Seek A game where you hide and call your dog's name to help him to find you.

Housetraining Teaching your dog to relieve himself in a designated area.

Mixed Breed Dog A dog whose parents are different breeds.

Purebred Dog A special kind of dog created by breeding dogs with the same characteristics.

Treat A special food given to a dog to reinforce his good behavior.

Sit It is the most basic obedience command and it consists of having your dog sit with his bottom on the ground.

Sit/Stay It is a common obedience command that consists of having your dog remain in the sit position until you release him.

Socialized dog A dog that is exposed to other dogs and people from a young age and is comfortable in unfamiliar situations.

9. Quiz solutions and explanations

1. YES
   Dog outfits are especially made for dogs and they can be useful in some situations. For example, if it is raining, a raincoat can keep your dog dry. If it is cold outside and if you have a short-haired dog, the outfit can keep him warm. Outfits for making your dog look cute are also fine, if your dog enjoys wearing them.
   Doll outfits are not made for dogs and they can be uncomfortable or they can have buttons or decorations that can be a choking hazard for dogs.

2. NO
   Like humans, dogs can have bad days. The dog could have had a vaccination or an injury and he might not be as friendly as usual.

3. NO
   The majority of the dogs in a shelter are not there because they have problems, but simply because they did not fit the lifestyle of their previous family or because their previous owner was not able to sustain the cost of having a dog.

4. NO
   Chocolate is very toxic for dogs.
   Onion, avocado, grapes, raisins, nuts and greasy foods can also make a dog sick. Food with small, sharp bones, such as fish and poultry need to

be avoided because dogs can choke on the bones or the bones can splinter and hurt the dog.

5.NO

Wrestling is never a good game to play with a dog, especially if there are other friends playing. Your dog may think that you are in a dangerous situation and he may attack your friends to protect you.

Printed in Great Britain
by Amazon

17587266R00018